How Japanese
Is That

How Japanese Is That

Sead Mahmutefendic

To order additional copies of this book, contact:
Xlibris
800-056-3182
www.Xlibrispublishing.co.uk
Orders@Xlibrispublishing.co.uk
813420

Zu ken men arojfgejn in himel arajn
Un fregn baj got zu's darf asoj sajn?
Yiddish song

Can we go up to heaven
And ask God should it be so?

The story is based on an actual event that took place in Paris in the early 70s of the last century. An agency piece of news, in the 90s, reported that a selfsame real-life cannibal was elected member of the Japanese Parliament.

This is that story.

After reading, it feels as if God has grown tired of His piece of creation that he created on the sixth day of Genesis, and by moving out of His retarded images, He wants to give up on them forever.

1.

Straight from the gentle terrains of Sapporo, Yasuhiro Tsuru was to take off on a plane to Paris, and he would surely have done so had he not been prevented by a sudden telegram.

His father was informing him of his mother's death.

Instead on the plane, for which he had already booked a ticket, the very same evening he would be sitting by the window in the first class of shinkansen, which would bring him to the North Tokyo Railway Station in the early morning hours. Poor Yasuhiro would hop into the first taxi to take him home, just long enough to quickly change and put on the suit for such occasions. He would instantly return to the car which, after only about twenty minutes, would bring him to the mortuary, in front of which, due to his lateness, some were pretty much holding their breath, awaiting his arrival. Five more minutes left until the beginning of the funeral.

In the first line of the funeral procession, he saw his father between two women, each holding him under his arm. These were his mother's sisters, whom he had seen two or three times in his life. In recent years, mother had often mentioned them and complained about them. In doing so, she gossiped about them and strove to laugh as much as possible.

The priest was right behind the casket. At the height of his chest he held one hand upon the other.

In the middle of the room, placed on an iron cart, a coffin lay in a bunch of flowers. Fumiko Tsuru was seventeen days short of turning thirty-seven.

Yasuhiro was as sad as a dog. At hundred and forty centimeters tall and weighing fifty-one kilograms, he pegged along on his two toothpicks in a straight line with his father and aunts, just behind the coffin, still composed enough to keep the three of them at a decent distance.

As soon as Fumiko was lowered into the freshly dug pit and the gravediggers began throwing the first shovels of earth over her, Yasuhiro stepped to the edge of the grave and, with his knees bent together slightly to the side, he effeminately crouched to grab a small clod, crumble it between his fingers and throw it onto the cover of his mother's coffin. People walked past him and did the same. In the end, the gravediggers thrust the shovel, and began to faster throw the excavated soil in.

Just as the richly decorated and lacquered coffin disappeared under the mound of earth, a strong desire arose in the young man to evaporate from that place at once, that no one asked him anything, nor to think of anything now. He knew that it would not work that way, and that he had to be patient and restrain himself once more. He would have to withstand all the petit-bourgeois nonsense that follows the funeral.

Fumiko was an ardent Buddhist; for the love of her, he would have to endure all this.

The following evening, Yasuhiro bid a cold goodbye to his father, though, for the umpteenth time already, he had firmly been assured that he would not be shortchanged a single yen from the financial allowance in respect of his studies of medicine at the Sorbonne. Father's only condition was contained in a succinct, dull admonition that it better not fail and turn into the opposite of what it was all about. The father did not forget to mention to his son to keep his hands off politics and female creatures.

It was August, and at every turn Yasuhiro kept looking discreetly over his father's shoulder at the clock on the wall across from him, although he knew full well that the announcer, for some more time, would not invite passengers over the loudspeakers to enter the gate and start boarding the plane, which was about to take off for the capital of France.

Yasuhiro knew that his father was hesitant, and he very much understood the state he was in, he wanted to tell him something, but it was also clear to him that he had no courage or strength at all for such a thing, or that, simply, the time and place did not allow it.

Yasuhiro knew that it was about his mother.

They both knew it deuced well, and both damn cunningly contrived to avoid talking about her: the son lest the memory hurt him, and his father's justification without the presence of the other party would not be worth while, and the father to justify himself before himself and before his son, though he knew well that such justification would be just pissing in the wind. Yasuhiro even imagined in those moments that his father had wished for her end.

It's been almost a decade since, without his own guilt and secret intention, he had been a direct witness to a quarrel between his father and mother. As far as the hidden child could have guessed, the cause of the quarrel was some clerk from his father's company. Yasuhiro-senior swore to his wife on his son Yasuhiro-junior that there was nothing special between them that she imagined there was, except, perhaps, mutual fondness, which had never gone beyond the scope of businesslike politeness.

– If one nicely addresses a pretty woman, does it mean that flirting is already in the offing? – foaming at the mouth and with his legs wide apart like a pair of compasses for drawing a circle, he stood across from her next to their double bed.

Fumiko was unrelenting. As primary proof, she had a photograph from a business dinner in which that geisha was in her husband's embrace. With a generous bonus payment, Fumiko gave a firm promise to her private detective that she would forever keep his services in discreet memory and gratitude.

After three days of tedious quarrels and mutual reproaches for coldness and neglect, tears, open threats of suicide, blackmail of all kinds, hypocritical assurances that such things existed in any average modern marriage, all the way to the express warnings that divorce would still be the most sensible solution for them both, if only it would not bring him gossip, inconvenience at work and a decline in authority among business partners, which would inevitably call into question his career, and consequently the financial privileges the two of them had so far, in which they lived, and to which, after all, they had became quite accustomed.

– Let our marriage from now on rest solely on the reason of money – Yasuhiro senior said solemnly. "Since you intend to do so, there is no place for the heart here. But just know, that's what you wanted and that's what you set up. Shigenobu Kishimoto, the director of my company, could have hugged me the same way, but it would not have such consequences the way you intend to portray them."

Pint-sized that he was, he theatrically and powerlessly spread his hands. With great resignation, Fumiko noticed the wedding ring she gave him.

– Otherwise, I have no choice but to put a bullet in the barrel of a revolver, and the two of you to be reduced to beggary in a few years – he said at the end.

Fatigue, apathy, despair, and resignation to yet another insult on top of everything else, and apparently this last pathetic statement of his, made Fumiko finally shut up and stop sniveling, which to him – the fox – was sign enough that his marriage had once more been saved at that very moment.

More out of fear that they would notice him than out of curiosity of witnessing the quarrel between his parents, tucked between the door and the closet, little Yasuhiro waited in vain for his mother to say something. In his imagination of a child, he thought for a moment that his mother had already died from his father's many words.

– I must go to the company now – he heard his father's voice. "You surely need the money for a hairdresser. Come on, spruce up. We could go to some nice restaurant for dinner tonight. I'll call you from the office, so we'll agree on which one to go to, okay Fumi?"

Fumiko was silent and watching the bony and spidery fingers of her hands, resting dead in her lap.

As soon as his father went out, Yasuhiro, with a wistful smile, took a peek at his mother. He saw her sitting on the edge of their double bed. She sat with her profile to him, so he could now clearly see the sharp outline of her nose, lips and chin.

He wiggled out of there. The toy from his lap fell on the floor. The sound startled Fumiko. She turned to him. When she noticed him, he instantly saw her eyes widening as the cobra's eyes widen with anger because of someone's presence, he saw her lips curve before the crying that was about to come, and very soon. Ruffled feathers, shame, or what? She stood up as if scalded, raised herself erect as much as possible, with those two eggs of hers swelling out in the front. On him, all wretched, lay her gaze full of arrogance and contempt.

– This is where you have holed up, worm! – her voice rang metallically and dryly.

As much as she restrained herself to keep her voice composed, it still trembled from the three-day crying and from having constantly swallowed saliva. It was only now, truly, that she was on the verge of becoming hysterical.

In those days Yasuhiro-junior suffered like an animal. He did not know how to approach his mother, let alone comfort her in her torments. He could not find valid and convincing reasons for this. It seemed to him that if he had told her, it would have made her even angrier. One of those nights he sincerely wished to kill his father.

There was no doubt that Yasuhiro had always been terrified by smiling and cheerful people, and this constantly made him think that they were, in fact, sources of the unnecessary and exaggerated amounts of superficial kindness. He marked his father very early on in his habits, his methods of upbringing in which there was everything but most of all that which had upfront been devoid of human, intimate and sincere, though in its outward assumption it manifested itself as such. The constant learning of complaisance with the obligatory smile initially caused a certain confusion in him, which, not infrequently, bordered on inner coldness, collected restraint, and almost icy indifference.

One time, owing to a headache, when he was not in the mood for company at all, he, of his own accord, stayed alone in the room. After a while, his mother entered to ask him to come join the guests. He sought every way to avoid it, wishing his head would really hurt. But when he noticed that he was artfully telling lies to his naïve mother, he felt the terrible and cold emptiness filling him whole, and he instantly cursed himself and his instilled scruples and habits. He wished for finding that much courage and sincerity, and for it all to be harmonious, so that he could dash among those distinguished, respected and highly esteemed guests, led by his fabulous and smiling father, who already had one eye on him (he knew that look very well), glancing nervously and waiting for him to appear at the salon door.

And what was he to do?

He was surprised by the fact that he could come up with these ideas at all. Could it be a dream? Anything can happen in a dream...

After all, he was brought up to keep his eyes cast down and speak softly.

He swore at himself with indignation. He scolded his heart for that momentary verbal debauchery and temporary determination.

His mother was standing before him. A silent plea on her face to come with her to the salon, among the guests. Only three days had passed since his father had convinced her of the tactlessness and impracticability of the divorce, and that because of some geisha, she would fall into disfavor and financial troubles.

Yasuhiro noted that she had suffered a lot these days. She, of course, tried to cover it up with a smile and makeup. However, anyone who looked more closely into her eyes would see that they were shaded with sadness and fatigue from sleepless nights.

– Shiro, I am so bored out there without you – she said.

Fumiko was on the verge of crying.

He realized that he would relent to her demands, because she was *so bored out there without him.* All of them were so bored, and despite all that, they smiled and made faces like wooden Russian dolls, and ran their doggy eyes over so that they would dig a grain from Fumiko's eyes, shaded with the sadness of sleepless nights, but also with her indomitable attentiveness and feigned hospitality.

Unhappy and lonely people smile. Neither their anger, nor their laughter – neither has either soul or justification.

Yasuhiro closed his eyes, inhaled, and followed his mother. Through semi-consciousness he registered her warning to once again apologize to their guests for his headache, for which he had already imagined of having truly troubled him a little, apologizing to himself for the pretense, and father, right upon having seen the last guest out, would talk to him about it in detail.

He is father, thought Yasuhiro-junior, he is what he is. In the end, what does he have to do with his father's flirtation? If anyone is affected therewith, it must be mother. If she forgave him, why does he have to make a fuss and poke about it? It is a matter between just the two of them. His was to heed and duly pass the school test and that with grades as high as possible.

All in tears Yasuhiro laughed.

The guests gathered in the salon welcomed him with icy indifference. One of them got up from his seat and approached the boy who was watching them with no interest at all. He grabbed him by the ends of his shirt. He tried to rip them apart, but failed to succeed in his intentions. It was apparent that he was putting in a lot of effort.

– What do you want to do? –Yasuhiro-junior asked.

– I want to see you naked in front of this esteemed gathering – the not-meant-to-be ripper of his shirt replied to him.

Those few torn shreds Yasuhiro held against his body so that they would not hang and his nakedness be revealed. With utter dismay, he felt trembling all over, not from the cold but from the vulgarity of the one whose fingers on himself he watched as if they were the legs of a poisonous spider. His sore spots were tingeling.

And then, all of a sudden, all those faces reverted from stony indifference to the usual, learned, simple kindness, and indefatigable smiles spiced up by the countless handshakes and upper-body bowing at the waist.

In the rear of the salon, he noticed his father, and a bit further, his mother, both crawling between the legs of the guests. Myriads of black cockroaches began creeping on the floor. The guests were smiling, and mother and father, with their mouths agape, were in pursuit of the scared bugs around themselves.

They used their fingers only if some of the bugs intended to escape into the hole in the floor or at the bottom of the wall.

As soon as the guests noticed what the two of them were interested in, every single one of them knelt down, pulling their trouser legs slightly up, so as not to wear them thin at the knees or destroy the sharp-ironed crease in the middle. It was obvious that the game was giving them too much joy, and that it made them quite cheerful.

Seeing that all the holes in the wall and the floor were closed up, the cockroaches, without any fear, began to enter their ears, eyes, nasal cavity, depending on what was closest to them and what they perceived as their nearest salvation.

The laughter instantly abated. One after another, the guests started to tip over on their back as if they were bugs. Most of them vomited. In their spits, the doused cockroaches were wriggeling their legs and fled in all directions to the same holes through which they had recently entered.

Yasuhiro noticed that father and mother were more and more shrinking. With considerable horror, he determined that the two of them now resembled cockroaches. Surprised by such a scene, he could not come to his senses for a long time and shake off that terrifying image and, finally, the thought that his parents had become two black crusty cockroaches. Benumbed and riveted to his spot, he watched dazedly those two insects, facing each other, touch one another with their huge, long antennae. Male and female. He concluded this by the size of their bodies. He assumed his mother was somewhat rounder and stockier.

He went towards them. The two cockroaches got terrified and started running each to its own side. He headed towards one of the two. He saw the round and stocky female escape into one of the holes, which were no longer closed up. He immediately turned to another cockroach. It was going straight for the hole and was just about to go in. Yasuhiro looked around to find a cloth or a newspaper. He couldn't see anything convenient for the occasion. But, just now, he noticed that he had lost his slipper in the recent scuffle. He was barefoot. How to step barefoot on a hideous cockroach? It would be even worse if it escaped into the hole.

He stepped quickly with his left foot, and then fully with his right foot in front of the hole, he blocked the cockroach. He felt something roundish against his sole. The crust popped and cracked under the weight of his leg, though he intended to do it as carefully as possible. He knew full well now that, under his sole, there was a smeared white and brown viscera of the bug. An expression of utter disgust appeared on his face and his lips stretched at once.

As soon as he removed his foot and saw the sticky and smeared cockroach stain on his sole, he immediately recalled that the stain could very easily be his father. His lips remained as stretched as they had been before, except that the glow in his eyes brightened up a bit. They became livelier, though he still felt some icy sadness within. As if he had rid himself of a huge burden, he kept on smiling with a vague expression on his face. As if he were saying to himself: "At last".

Then he woke up. At first, he couldn't figure out where he was. He looked around to find the window, so when he finally saw that it was behind him, he thought he was at his grandpa's and grandma's in

Shingū. Somewhat awake and still quite drowsy, he saw a cherry tree through the window. Only then did he realize that he was on the first floor of his family home.

The first flashes of dawn started appearing.

Yasuhiro felt terribly sleepy and broken. His eyelids were sticking to each other. His eyes were painful and somehow too tight. Then he felt a shiver from his recently ended dream. He thought that he would not be able to fall asleep again. He lowered the blinds on the window and returned to bed. And soon, he fell asleep again.

When he woke up and opened the windows wide, he saw on his watch that it would be noon soon. He recalled his dreams, appearances and apparitions of the previous night, and was a bit ashamed for them. He knew he couldn't end his father that way. He will have to choose another, and more efficient method. He would like to see him suffer, and not because of guilty conscience for he had never had one, but to see him go through physical pain and ask for forgiveness because of the offense he had caused his mother.

From that day on, Yasuhiro began to take revenge on his father with silence, which meant his open contempt for him.

His father knew this well now, and this was the main reason that Yasuhiro-senior, not even dead, would dare to mention his late wife's name before the bereft son. As he had long since lost even the slightest feeling for her, he found within himself a life-saving solution that it would be wisest not to tickle the dragon's tail or utter a single word about her. Hence the two of them cautiously and discreetly avoided the deceased's name as someone would avoid the plague, so most of the time their conversation was about the financing of Yasuhiro's studies at the Sorbonne, as well as the correctness of his identity documents, the verification of his checking accounts, the validity of the plane ticket, and so on and so forth, down to the tiniest details like the suitcase key sets, just not to get poor Fumiko into their conversation.

Finally, the announcer invited passengers over the loudspeakers to start for the plane that was to take off to Paris in about ten minutes.

Yasuhiro-junior bid a cold goodbye to Yasuhiro-senior. Tepidly held out hands were a convenient response to their firm and unbreakable friendship. They looked at each other indifferently.

Having mixed with the crowd of passengers packed at the boarding gate, junior never again turned to his senior. His meter and a half, with elevator shoe heels and vertical stripes on his suit, disappeared forever in the crowd of passengers.

In front of the airport building, in the parking lot, next to the open back door of a huge *mazda* of Yasuhiro-senior the shipbuilder, a liveried driver was waiting with a servile smile on his face and the obligatory deep bow at the waist towards his boss. Yasuhiro had no smile for him, the kind he was ready to give to anyone his affairs depended on. He did not have to bow as he was getting in the back of his limousine. His son's cold handshake was still pulsating unpleasantly in his mind. Still, he thought, this was his only son and the only thing left for him in this unhappy and unreliable world.

The slow and comfortable ride around Tokyo in the evening hours made him increasingly calm. He was thinking less and less about his son, who was now flying above the sea towards Beijing on the Air France plane. Remembering that he had a pre-arranged date with his *geisha* later that evening, he once again recalled Yasuhiro, but now, instinctively, as if he wanted to defend himself before him. A smile stretched just one end of his lip: "Europe will put this nonsense out of his head. Life must go on. Honor is for the dead, and life belongs to the living".

From the window seat, Yasuhiro-junior observed the clouds beneath him that resembled huge bales of cotton in the airless space. Night was falling. Down in the depths, he imagined the lit lights of Tokyo.

There are people down there, he thought. They cannot even be seen from here, but each of these amoebae has their own torments, sufferings and sad joys.

As a result of such thinking, he felt an unhealthy excitement. He kept thinking about what had happened to him in the past two days. Somehow, he handled it with more ease when things were there, within his grasp. Everything was behind him now: mother, father, memories, and Japan as well. Ahead of him was unknown Europe, which he only knew from textbooks of geography, and some of history too. He believed that his idea of it would change, but what it did all mean in relation to what at that moment he felt and saw beneath him through the window.

The moon was floating between the clouds, and its presence seemed to provoke and disturb him even more. To eliminate this unpleasantness and put an end to his discomfort, he turned to the interior of the plane, where, at that moment, a flight attendant was passing between the rows of seats and, with a decent smile, was offering hot beverages in plastic cups to the passengers.

Yasuhiro thanked her kindly. When she had passed him, he closed his eyes to once more try to fall asleep.

So, mom died. She is no more. Now I no longer have anyone. I lost my father a long time ago. I attribute this to myself as my conscious act against which I did nothing to have it reconsidered. The only, and my biggest sin is that I continue to take his money. My hypocrisy is greater than his, because I keep doing what I ostensibly blame myself for. Or perhaps it is better to turn this around: why should these facts bother me? Since he is my father, and he did not prove to be such to me, why should it not be returned in kind? After all, he won't even feel it, on the contrary, it will give him an illusion that our relationship can go on, so why shouldn't I let him have it? Thus, things stay the same; he thinks that my stuff will pass in time, and I... I, it seems, start not to think. I do not think. Yasuhiro Tsuru-junior no longer thinks... I am, after all, a tiny louse and a coward. I like babbling a bit against my daddy, but I would still suck his money dry.

How idiotically one intends to release oneself from the sense of responsibility before one's own conscience!

Do I have any conscience at all when I still have the strength and the will to reframe things and make them such, so as to give me an excuse before it? It's a deception then. It is far more painful and sad if we are unable to find the way from our brain to our heart than when a man does it to another man. But if I truly think this way, then it is at the same time cruel and raw to accept such things.

That night, drowsy Yasuhiro did not fall asleep, and he naturally decided to stand in defense of his thoughts, not finding them sufficiently discursive but more intuitive. Even if he were wrong, he would easily attribute it to physical exhaustion and nervous tension. Oh, how hard these past two days have been.

He blinked several times from drowsiness with his wrinkled and puffy eyelids. His eyes were tremendously strained. He tried counting some sheep, the clearer picture of which he could not imagine. It was only then that he remembered that he had never even seen a single sheep except in an agricultural TV series and one Georgian film.

All his efforts were in vain, nothing helped.

He cast another glance out the window. The moon was no longer there. The clouds had already dispersed. Down on the ground, nothing could be made out. Down there, people breathe and sleep, kill and love each other, and the two hundred or so of us on this plane are flying over them like small flies in the dark above the potato bug that does its work immersed in the crown of potato flowers. No one will find it a good idea to die laughing at all this, because man has long forgotten what happiness is, what all this nonsense called the life of a living being is, and why man has surrounded himself with the unnatural so that it seems totally natural to him, and feels safe as if being in a stone tower the keys of which he has long since lost.

Maybe they are flying above the forests of Siberia? Maybe above a sea where some fish must eat someone today or soon be someone's food themselves. People and animals are in the forests, fish are in the sea. Respectable shipbuilder Yasuhiro Tsuru-senior's son flew to Europe to study medicine at the Sorbonne. The father is probably already with some geisha. The smart and promising son gets smart and racks his brains about it on the Air France plane, and mother Fumiko lies at lot 120 in the family tomb number 53, and all that appertains to the image of a good and well-known family.

A nice, wealthy and smiling family. All we have to do is dig out the samurai roots from somewhere, and if they would genetically be linked to the seven from Kurosawa's film, that would be the right thing then. The samurai, the father with geishas, the mother in lot number 53, and the son studying medical science at the Sorbonne.

Ç'est fantastique! Ç'est formidable! Ç'est drôle![1]

Ç'est merde! Oh, mon Dieu![2]

Some idiotic thoughts were rolling in Yasuhiro's head, he thought superficially, sentimentally and unctuously, and in fact he was so tired, unhappy, drowsy and nervous that it made his intense thoughts instantly burst like taut strings and disappear like soap bubbles. And

1 *Fr.* – It's fantastic! It's splendid! It's funny!
2 *Fr.* – It's shit! Oh, my God!

then, suddenly, he felt the horror and an icy shudder crawl up his spine and arms. He broke out in a cold sweat. He would like to die.

Someone was shaking him by the shoulder. He couldn't come to his senses at once. He was scared and he couldn't understand where he was. In front of him, he saw that same face of the flight attendant and her lovely, professional smile like on a poster at the tourist bureau. He noticed that her lips were moving like they move on Japanese postcards when viewing the face from different angles.

As if those lips were about to convey something important to him?

The hostess continued to move her lips, depending on the angle Yasuhiro was watching her from, but he could not understand her at all. A bit of hubbub wafted to him as well as the metallic announcer's voice through the loudspeakers.

That totally woke him up.

– Where are we now? – he asked the flight attendant.

Notified of the upcoming landing, passengers were strapping their seatbelts. He realized that they would land somewhere in a few moments.

From the powerful engines, nothing could be heard of what the flight attendant was saying to him. He noticed that she had thick bangs on her forehead in a straight line, trimmed right above the eyebrows. One of her eyes tended to move to the side a bit, and that only when she smiled so kindly. Her gaze was likewise kind and likeable.

The indicator lights went on. Yasuhiro tried to play with the illusion, such as, was truly this aluminum of a plane in Japan yesterday and now already in France?

However, in the formed crowd, this ceased to interest him.

The glowing letters warned passengers to do as stated in the instructions. At the same time, the announcer's even voice was chattering in French and English in turns. Passing between the rows of seats, the flight attendant stopped beside him. With a Barbie smile she told him: "We have just landed at Orly!"

2.

Paris, 20 October 1970

A few days ago, I arrived in Paris. Nothing remarkable except the fact that I happily passed all those landings and stops at the transit airports from which Europeans suffer more than we Japanese do. We seem to have greatly surpassed them in that, though I would not dare attribute this to our proverbial speed as much as to their healthier sense and understanding of time, which they have so much ahead of them, that moving the clock hands a whole hour forward or a whole hour back, according to them, means absolutely nothing special. As a man who, in a way, has begun entering the pores of their habits, I feel that there is a certain special charm in this. I have not yet found the much-needed peace and time to think about it in more detail, as well as about some completely new ascents of my soul. This, I think, is first and foremost influenced by the new impressions and new ideas that I come across on a daily basis. In this matter, I must forbid myself to value the things that are happening to me now by our Japanese standards and parameters, as in that case they would surely become messy and lose their original meaning and reason, not allowing me the opportunity to place them where they truly belong. Even if make a mistake, I will have to use the standards of these people, first of all, these are the facts that they view the thing the way it looks to me in their line of sight, and judge it the way their reason and fear suggest.

Paris, 17 December 1970

Apart from doing my regular study duties, that is, going to listen to the lectures, and performing scheduled exercises in certain subjects, nothing special happened to me during these two Parisian months.

I wouldn't write about Paris like this right now, one cannot even write about it. I'm beginning to admire more and more all those penmen, who sit down in front of a blank piece of paper with the illusion that they will manage to depict what they feel about this city to some of their readers. I can only be genuine in my malice if I write that the Seine, the Prévert's Seine, the green Seine from the postcard, is so dirty with mud and faeces. I didn't see any of the tramps I had read about in the books. There is also the famous Eiffel Tower, which people climb in a huge elevator for two crucial reasons only: to see the sea of rooftops beneath them and to try to sense the end of infinite Paris somewhere on the far horizon, or to stare from above into the depth underneath, again for two prosaic reasons: how some may have dared to step over this fence and jump into the abyss, or - why would not they do it at least once in their lives, since we only live once anyway.

Touching the ground happens in a thousandth of a second. One would neither be aware of it nor feel it. By the time this whole mechanism of pain transmission through the nerves to the center in the brain is completed, the matter is pretty much over: man has taken himself off the agenda for good.

However, the trouble is that most of these intentions remain solely an afterthought, and remain hanging like a tuft of fog, so that man no longer belongs either to those who are still in life or to those who have left it. From that point on, he just floats and keeps quiet. He had already met with doubt, he recognized it, embraced it and made a decision. That decision became irrevocable. After that, death can only be a postponement. The thought of death becomes so intoxicating that it begins to be an obsession. It provokes desire. The desire for death is always in us. Death should not come as a surprise, but something ordinary that inevitably awaits us at the end of our journey and visit in this life. Death is sobering.

If anything is left to our decision, our will and freedom, it is that we can choose what our death will be, and not that it chooses what our end will be. Only death can wake us up and bring us back from the nightmare.

Paris, 20 December 1970

Two months have passed. In the main, I spend all this time alone, except for a few casual and unimportant acquaintances. Such atmosphere I created around myself not because I wanted so, but because I couldn't find a way to approach anyone. The reason for that, I believe with considerable certainty, is the feeling of hurt because of my dwarfishness. Beside that, over time, an insurmountable shame has crept into me.

How many times I have cursed it. How does it feel to draw the last atoms of your healthy and cheerful spirit from within to give yourself some kind of impetus and convince yourself that it doesn't mean anything special, while at the same time you have to do it all with such nonchalance so that you don't feel in it any intention, self-deception or breaking the mirror, which clearly gives you a reflection of your ugly face and deformed body. That sense of self-struggle, from self-contempt to painful masochism only to comfort yourself that you are honest and aware of all that you carry as an indelible seal of your ill-fated destiny.

It is useless to say what it matters that you are short and ugly, you are smart and rich, you can have anything, you can buy anything. There are times when it seems to me that this is how it can truly be. Then I feel flattered because I think it might be so, and I start jumping around the apartment with some wild rapture and enthusiasm.

After that, I sit, calm down and try to properly picture to myself that this cannot be true. How could I have distorted something in such an ugly way and drawn the wrong conclusion?

I try to despise myself the way I am. I still feel that the recent mood in me hasn't quite gone away. Indeed, that's when I think that intelligence and wealth are enough to make a man happy.

Naught!

Somehow, it's even tolerable while I'm in the subway crowd or in line in front of the cinema. However, the fact that there is a decimeter between me and the first man in the crowd is enough to instantly notice in someone's eyes the kind of human gaze that hurts and offends more than being stabbed in the stomach. When, from all that moves, goes around him, from all the people, the shop windows, the impressions offered to his eyes and poor soul, he finds just me as the most interesting to him. If at least in those eyes there were some disdain, or pity. Those eyes only say: "God still keeps even such ones on earth, doesn't He?"

All such looks can take one to the fence of the Eiffel Tower.

And then that shame. You don't know what's worse: either that or that powerless, irrational anger! Careless curiosity infuriates you. You say to yourself that he wouldn't have stared at you if you had been of a normal stature.

Why isn't he watching others?

Others are not slant-eyed like you.

It's not because of my slant eyes but because of my stature.

The shopkeeper from behind the window of a charcuterie[3] is smiling.

– You too – I yell at him through the glass – you too are a pig like everyone else. Don't you know that with that look you have wrecked my whole day! Look at the others, look at the hat, look at female derrières if you are not gay and not at my meter and a half of height. Your eyes tell me that my new lustrine suit is as if on a puppet.

Um, I see!... I've already started imagining things a lot. This is my pure fabrication. I have never noticed anyone watching me from behind the shop window of any charcuterie, let alone have I angrily shouted through the glass such words addressing him with - *toi*. I would never allow myself such insolence.

I'm sitting at the table in the dining room. I'm writing this diary. I feel that unpleasant shame rising again. It knocks first. I watch it through the peephole for a little while, but then I dare to open the door, because I'm aware that I will eventually have to do it.

– Come on in – I tell it. – I see that you came to me, torture me if it pleases you.

It enters me, I feel it.

How nice it is without it. That's when I feel such bliss, and I think I'm going to go crazy with happiness right away. It usually lasts longer. I am sure if it were not for it, my imagination would not give me more momentum.

I don't see anyone, and I don't care about anything, everything goes my way: I merge the continents and mountains with my own hands, uncover the seas and the oceans, move armies, and I'm two

---

3 *Fr.* – A delicatessen specializing in dressed meats and meat dishes.

hundred meters tall. Underneath I see some tiny dots that are moving like under the lens of a microscope. They move from one place to another. Then I tell myself: We, Yasuhiro Tsuru-junior, are the highest, the most powerful and the strongest! What more do I need than that belief? Every thought pervades me and I do not doubt a single one of them. Why would I doubt? There is no resistance or derision from anywhere.

Why isn't someone looking at me pityingly then?

What imbues my whole soul is the rapture, which only a little later I most seriously begin to fear. It becomes so enormous that it starts to torment and pressure me dreadfully. Experience tells me that it cannot be everlasting, but that it comes, first of all, to inebriate me, then to sway me in the widest of amplitudes, and later on it suddenly disappears while I gradually sober up from it and begin to torture myself again, without finding any better solution. All I need at that time is sleep and I beckon it like a desperate man beckons his hope. That shame of mine comes again, but now already combined with fear, and the more I'm afraid, these two transcend me and threaten to engulf me and have me simply drown in them. When I emerge again and swim out of their damn water, I remain completely alone for a while, and then hatred takes up their place.

Imagine living with it. It gives you neither peace nor pleasure, and it systematically destroys you. You must feed it as some vicious parasite, which is to devour you over time if you stop deceiving yourself with it.

I have never publicly expressed hatred for another person. The reason for this I find mostly in my innate shame and fear that I will not be thought of nicely.

I cannot stand it anymore between these two contradictions. I know for sure that they will one day have to encounter each other unlike the previous situations when they luckily and skillfully missed each other. Thus – as the Europeans say – everything will fall into place. The boss of the house will be known.

I dread the moment of that encounter.

I often wish my mother were here with me. I never remember my father. I have the need to put my head in the lap of the first person I meet in the cinema, the cafe, the park, and have it rest there for a long time. To keep quiet, to cry... I would give all the wealth to someone letting me have this. That's what mother used to do when father was not home for long. I was happy for her, and she was unhappy about father. I didn't care that neither of them was unhappy about me. I would come to her to lay my head in her lap. She would caress me for a long time, running her fingers through my soft hair, which gave me pleasant goosebumps. She would do that until I fell asleep immersed in her lap. Her caresses and my restrained crying, the dreariness in the house because of father's nightly absences with some geishas, all supported my childish premonition that something inhumane was going on between them. I felt her suffering the most, and for the same reasons I suffered no less, although even then I knew quite well that for father's fake and feigned smile she would be able to push me aside at once. It did not prevent me from truly feeling the extent of her pain. On such nights, shame for her suffering and anger for father's callousness were becoming ingrained in me for keeps. Why did she let him hurt her in such a way?

These questions troubled me for a short time only. She was a witty woman. She no longer imagined the world but invented it. She would sit me down beside her, wipe away both our tears, begin to smile forcedly and spuriously until I followed suit. That's when I perceived the splendor of her soul. This woman made fun of everything and regarded everything around her, except her marriage, in the upside-down dimension. I would run out of tears, but shame would occur at tunes. It was a reminder that something was wrong. I sensed that my mother, this once, was trying with utmost effort to make things up and, with time, it became sadder to listen to her and look at her so lovable and unhappy.

It would also happen that father would find us like that. Mother would suddenly go quiet, then *continue* talking to me about my school. I would clearly remain dumbfounded and confused with her sudden change of the topic of conversation, which my father would notice with open indignation and mockingly laugh at her clumsy deception.

– You're lying and cheating as always – he would say to her face.

She would get so excited, flushed and tongue-tied at that remark that her hands would instantly start shaking.

Father brought uneasiness among us. Over time, she completely stopped waiting for him. Her resentment for him was also gone. What is more, I now think she wanted him to stay out of the house as long as possible and leave us alone as much as possible to get drunk with our play and imagination.

So, mother would go quiet and, ashamed, get up from her chair and leave us both without greeting. I felt that she strived, and she was doing her best, to feign serenity so that he would not cajole her into outpours of anger and repressed jealousy. But what she was hiding back then got completely transposed and instilled into me.

Shame over mother and fear over father.

Instead of her, I felt it. At first, I carried that burden with some defiant pride, but over time it began weighing down on me so much that I felt an increasing contempt and dubiety for the two of them, who elegantly and tacitly let their loathsome acts pass, and without shame and hesitation fed their stench into me. I think I have started stinking from that kind of stench ever since.

Paris, 14 February 1971

First of all, a few words should be said about what Miss Dominique Lemaire is like.

She is an ugly girl. But this does not in any way put me off, because I find that she is exactly the one who, in a certain way, could compensate in me for my increasingly manifested complex due to my dwarfish stature, which has caused me a lot of inconvenience lately.

Namely, Dominique and I are in the same group for exercises in pathology. Her last name starts with an *L*, and mine with a *T.* At first, we didn't even know each other, so to speak. I constantly kept myself at a distance from my male and female colleagues, though I used all possible means to make it unnoticeable. I was ready to help anyone who needed my help. With polite nods and pleasant smiles, I accepted other people's thoughts, agreed with suggestions, though most of them I could not adopt for myself at all.

To what end, then, such trait of mine, that is the question!

And none of this would be worth mentioning if they had not watched me closely throughout that game. It was obvious that they were amused and intrigued by such my *Japanese* behavior, to which, in the absence of more correct solutions, they eagerly ascribed the overtone of exoticism, the mystique of the Far East, Zen Buddhism and who knows what else these Europeans are able to label us with, just so they wouldn't have to be silent and wouldn't have to admit that they haven't got a clue about anything, which not a single person would hold against them. This way...

However, the truth was that my colleagues in the group could never have guessed that they had been rejected by my upbringing since I could not adapt to them. Often, through such my actions, I put myself in the position of sensing on the face of the one I talk with, what should be said: yes, with a smile or not, I agree with everything he says, both for my *certain peace* and for his vanity because I *am carefully listening* to him. I knew that this game was about to take on a certain shape, because our relationships have reached the limit when we inevitably had to open the door to one another and finally let each other into our lives.

I believe it all started with one exercise where we were tasked with dissecting an old man's corpse.

Everyone in the room, and there were about fifteen of us, felt quite nauseated and uneasy as we stood surrounding professor Robert Le Blanche. To dispel the anxiety in us – most likely that's what it was – he began with an experiment quite unconventionally: "First of all, ladies and gentlemen, I have to necessarily emphasize one thing at the very beginning of this exercise, which is that not a single one of you here present will ever be a good, not to say, perfect doctor, if one does not have, and only later unite, the two most essential traits of our profession – first, sharp eyes like a hawk, and second, any absence of disgust at things into which you put your hands and with them your scalpel too. I want to say, if Mother Nature has not endowed you with these instruments or, if by any chance you have not received it with the first mother's milk, then it is much smarter and more sensible for you, while it is not too late, to take your majesties to Cardin, Yves Saint Laurent, or to apply as an apprentice at one of the jewelers on Boulevard Haussmann, than to stick your little noses in the buttocks of all sorts of oldsters like this unlucky one, right in front of us."

Our silence was the best and clearest reply.

The old man's corpse was placed prone on the table with a sheet-metal plate. Professor Le Blanche solemnly lifted his right hand up, theatrically stretched his forefinger like an alchemist in medieval graphics, and quickly, in a wondrous semi-ellipse, lowered it to the cadaver's behind, passing it utterly nonchalantly between the buttocks. His fist did not stop there, but kept uselessly circling in the air, something like an unwound thread, until that same index finger stopped in front of his very lips.

The freshmen in attendance watched this sudden exhibition with utmost attention in solemn and tense silence. Before anyone could even come to their senses from astonishment of what they had just seen, the professor opened his frog-like mouth wide, stuck his tongue out and licked his finger from root to fingertip. Only then did he turn his eyes to us and then took out a cloth from his pocket and wiped the saliva off his finger.

One girl was caught so as not to fall to the ground while losing her consciousness, and at the same moment another one, with jam jar bottom glasses, turned her head and began to vomit on the floor, as if she were at a steamboat railing with the raging sea underneath.

The professor was silent and exultant. It is quite clear that he had the obvious intention of putting to the test how the two *essential traits of our profession* needed to be a good doctor function. He cast an ironic glance at those fussing over the unconscious medical student. Three hairs from the back of his head were, with the help of hair gel, successfully put up to his very forehead where primarius Le Blanche, MD MSc, got them tangled up in a real bunch of some six or seven, possibly even eight hairs. Small and stocky that he was, he sat on a chair with utmost complacency, joined his fists in his lap, spreading and pulling together something that looked like legs. He hopped with his feet a couple of times, significantly and measuredly, along with nodding, his glaze gliding from one student to the other.

I don't know why this thought came to me at that moment: Such ones are the best in doing those things with women only because they have a paranoid fear that if they don't do so, the women will cheat on them with the first one who comes along.

Then I noticed that more people put their hand to their mouth. This time, it seemed to me, it was disingenuous. They acted as if they could vomit at any moment and in such manner give their personal effect to the professor's performance and his morbid wittiness and bizarreness. Some giggled, while others watched this surgical operetta most seriously. Well, most of us were still holding open notebooks in our hands and waiting for something important the professor would say to us and what we would write down.

I, however, was among those who had not yet found the time to properly respond to the professor's unexpected gesture. Mister professor Le Blanche instantly cast his quick and vainglorious glance over us once more, to which, as we could immediately notice, he attached particular scientific and pedagogical significance. It was evident that he enjoyed the situation his action had brought us into.

– Alors, ladies and gentlemen, you could see for yourselves to what the various circumstances in our venerable profession compel Hippocrates' followers. I would not like to abuse your valuable patience and repeat to you all what I have just told you. Please, who would be so brave and kind to demonstrate in front of everyone what I have just done?

There was complete silence in the hall now. In such atmosphere, there was something simultaneously sad and funny about looking at the cadaver, who was the only remaining indifferent to and unimpressed by this whole experiment. One of the fifteen of us was about to put a finger between his two shriveled buttocks and then lick it in front of everyone. In order for a man not to show disgust, he would also have to laugh to convince others that hence he would most likely become a first-rate doctor. You simply had to lick your finger with such nonchalance as if you were just licking ice cream while walking down Champs-Elysees. This would for sure provoke a genuine outburst of giggling, the professor's favor, and on the other hand, give the demonstrator the repute of the one who can stomach anything.

I felt an extraordinary feeling begin growing inside me, which increasingly dissolved and melted me. I sensed that this was what sooner or later had to come: to show something before others, to arouse their attention, to confuse, to shock. I don't know, it seems I had always been waiting for that.

So, something had to be done when they were least expecting it. Now was a good time, I am the one who must do it, even if it gives rise to malicious and derisive gossip. The reason may be in the fact that everything then – and precisely then – terribly got on my nerves, the professor's predominance and arrogance, his histrionic and repulsive egocentrism, and all of that was garnished by his shallow and superficial self-satisfaction.

Intellectual onanism.

At the very beginning of the experiment, I noticed a huge mirror on the wall in which he observed himself every moment. His uvular «r» triggered my stomach pain. As if he were in a phonetic exercises class, stressing and drawling each syllable as when Georges Pompidou almost burst into tears a couple of months ago on TV screens on the occasion of de Gaulle's death, in front of the indifferent French: "La France est veuve!"[4]

All of this made our professor-narcissist swagger like a Gallic rooster in front of his hens.

I have to step forward, I told myself. The rebels and the brave always provoke reproach or favor. Mostly never indifference. The

---

4 *Fr.* – France is a widow.

former is certain to affect me, the latter I may possibly provoke in them.

None of those present in the room meant anything special to me. Their general favor was enough for me. I know that in an instant I decided to try what professor Le Blanche had just done in front of us all.

I felt someone's fingers on my loin. Someone was pushing a finger into my back.

No one seemed to be ready for such a disgusting and nauseous act. That is why my raised hand came as a good excuse to them for masking their own fear before the swaggering professor. As much as a sense of uneasiness was present, there was so much fear in them, and thus their hypocrisy of medicine emerged to the surface. So, I had to use that advantage over them.

Strangely enough, I was not particularly excited about what I had to do, nor was I ashamed of what I thought about then. Hatred and disgust made me go to the corpse. I also noticed that the professor was caught off-guard by my determination and courage. He hoped, perhaps, that some Frenchman would do it, not some pint-sized Japanese with slant eyes. Only now, when I recall the sequence of events, do I realize the vicious mockery that will have double-crossed me and made fun of me before these smug medical gentry.

To avoid all the theatricality that my next gesture could be very easily accompanied by, I straightaway stuck my finger in the cadaver's behind, licked it, and wiped it off with the same cloth that the professor had previously laid down next to the corpse.

I returned to the same spot among my colleagues. This time I nearly stumbled from some festive excitement. My ill-fated fear was coming back into me, and with it – I knew it quite well – shame will have ambled soon.

Many of my colleagues did not even notice what I had actually done. They were now nudging each other, stretching their necks and wondering what had happened with me. The only one who had closely and carefully followed my deed was professor Le Blanche. With measured steps, he approached the front row of students, meaningfully holding his hands clasped on his behind. The row disjoined to let him pass. Now he had only me before him.

He unclasped his hands. With a showbiz motion of a ruthless, insensitive, self-infatuated and complacent man, he grabbed my hand with his hand and lifted them together over our heads like a boxing judge does with the winner's hand.

– Dear colleague – he said as if announcing something important on the first RTF channel – you truly have one great trait so important for a top doctor. You don't seem to be a queasy person at all. That will be great in your career, I say, and I congratulate you on that with all my heart. Unfortunately, however, I have to mention one thing that does no credit to your doctoral honor. You simply do not possess an evolved gift of observation, because (here he raised his voice and started shouting at the top of it), you did not notice that I had stuck one finger in the deceased's behind, and licked quite another.

As soon as he said that, he turned his back on me in one vigorous semicircle like a general. For a while, he held his right hand up and his index finger stretched as if he intended to wag at someone with it. Only then did I notice that the general was looking at himself in that mirror on the opposite wall.

I suppose that poor general Le Blanche did this finger demonstration every year, in a similar manner our school photographer, every year before blinding us with his flashlight, would stare at the cross with his huge eyes, which would cause a storm of laughter and cheering from the students. By the way he performed it, and later reported the results, it could be concluded that it served him pretty much as a joke, which he sought to conveniently fit into the introductory part of the practice in pathology.

Without affectation and in an old man's manner, he laughed long and earnestly to tears. He was choking with laughter. He pulled out a handkerchief to wipe away the tears teeming in the corners of his eyes. Most of my notable colleagues simply competed as to who would more faithfully imitate professor Le Blanche. Some were grinning forcibly, pulling all sorts of grimaces on their faces, and some had no bounds at all so they even grasped their bellies and pretendedly stooped.

The only thing that put the brakes on this travesty was the exaggeration of professor Le Blanche himself.

It was already high time for the giggling and time-wasting to come to an end. He did not seem to think so. I find that in such kind of people, laughter, at the end of a successful prank, can easily turn into embarrassment. They do not know how to say: "Listen young man, I hope you will not take this amiss and get mad at me. The trap was for everyone, and the fact that you fell into it should teach you to be more careful in the future. I give you the opportunity, as well as your colleagues, to settle the score with me during your studies. Please, test my sense of humor. Don't just set me up with some teenager, the rest I accept as fun on my account. A joke should be distinguished from a travesty."

Speaking of travesty, it was here only towards the cadaver. My pride, vanity and anger did not allow me to fit into the general mood, and thus I chose our lovely, Japanese, smiling as the safest shield. I can only imagine how I looked even stupider in their eyes.

The laughter could not last forever. The dead man (who knows how the wretch ended), the laughter around him. The fear and anxiety of the corpse were completely gone.

This is a man. That is, this was once a man. I felt him now as closest to me of all the living present. Why do such nice words come out about people? They, by their very instinct, do what the legal and aesthetic norms are intended to deny them. What is missing is being objected to. So, should that what is missing be declared a human trait? People are being told to love and respect, to not pollute the air to others, because history has taught its readers that is what we have least of and what is missing. Thus, the history of man, on the one hand, and the arts and sciences, on the other, are like two rail tracks that will never be joined, and that are traveled by a strange protoplasm called man. It is their destiny to go side by side, that their signposts from the Neanderthal to the astronaut are followed by man, supported by the same illusions, absurdities, anguish and futility on the way to ultimate doom and eternal darkness. Some are here to use their heads for various ideas, die for them, renounce them, then grab with their claws totally new ones, while others are here to indifferently brush all of that aside to *live out their lives*, and in the moments of instinctive call of the living matter, at beck and call of someone cunning, they jump like a rabid dog at the first one pointed to them.

What is what in this mysterious world? What is death? Is this corpse joking with us? Who is putting their finger in whose behind?...

I waited for the laughter to subside. The last to stop was professor Le Blanche. His eyes were red and still wet with tears. He was constantly blowing with certain happy rapture and excitement.

When he saw me without any expression on my face, he approached me, put his hand on my shoulder and patted me: "You, my colleague, do not be angry with me. I assure you that there was no ill intent. After all, admit it, you volunteered. Anyone could have been in your place."

I was completely resigned. I felt somewhat similar while parting with my father at the airport. I thought: I'll have to do my best to keep my troubles to myself here as well.

The professor quickly and cunningly squinted at me. I straightened up as much as I could. Even so, I did not reach to the shoulders of the closest person. Nonetheless, being hurt gave me strength and advantage over all these buffoons.

The professor became serious at once. He looked at me openly, and asked me directly and unequivocally: "You didn't get mad at me for this, did you? I ask you most kindly to leave no room for such possibility."

– What if I am mad? – I asked him a question as my answer. – What do you think medicine is? Two future letters for vanity, a white coat, a temperature list in clean hands. Medicine is this corpse here that has already begun to decay. It should remind us how helpless our heads are, and yet, despite everything, we are so complacent, vain, and beyond bounds of good taste in love with our humble selves and our insignificance. Not only should one touch it with a finger, but one should eat it if necessary without vomiting while doing so. I believe no one here will take me literally. Medicine is not a beauty salon for ladies and gentlemen, it is love, tear, and pain over someone else's anguish, the meat industry, cannibalism, reeking shit, hot urine, all of it under the title of man we long since began being disgusted with but did so broad-mindedly and generously choose this craft. A doctor is one-hundred billionth leukocyte who, along with others, fights against everything that intends to destroy man. And just one more thing: How could I not get mad with this whole circus you had set up so that one of us medical freshmen (and freshman means – wet behind the ears) would turn out to be a clown. Is that how you gain reputation among your future colleagues?

– If anyone, I first of all should be the one to get mad, because you have not shown that you are able to combine the two elemental traits that every excellent doctor should have in his genes – said professor Le Blanche.

– If you consider yourself to be such an excellent doctor, which obviously you are not (provided I use the same criteria that you used and which – by the way – I do not believe at all), let me note that you yourself did not notice that I had done the same as you. The same self-confidence with which we had observed you, backfired on you while you were observing me. I did not know about your deceit, and you, having deceived us, myself included, could not have assumed that I would do it to you in the same way. I did not expect your deceit, and you did not expect mine. We are thus equal in this. Do you see any logic in that?

– What logic? – professor Le Blanche tried to surprise me, obviously all confused.

– That a lie can be truer than the greatest truth – I calmly replied.

My words made a strong impression on the attendees. These were completely different faces now. No one was grinning at me anymore.

The slant-eyed, dwarfish Japanese.

The professor was silent for a while. Then he took a step back and stood on my right. He looked at me carefully from head to toe.

– Bravo! Bravo! Bravissimo. Consider that you passed the exam in my subject. You have fascinated me. I think you will be a remarkable pathologist!

I have always been terrified by cheerful and smiling people.

– You just took the liberty of stating that I will be a bad doctor – I replied to him calmly. – Only if you do not consider medicine to be the science responsible only for determining a man's death.

– But you said you had tricked me – said the professor.

– Then I'm a trickster, not a pathologist.

– That's also a requirement for a good pathologist – mister Le Blanche was a bit confused.

– Provided the corpse has agreed to this type of deception.

– This is Zen – I heard someone whisper from the group.

– Merde! – I heard another voice.

– This is true Zen!

– Is that Zen? – the professor asked me most seriously.

– The biases that you Europeans have – I answered, looking him straight in the eye. – Everything you do not understand about the Japanese, you designate as Zen, as if it were an exotic plant.

The guys and girls warmed up to me. Some even approached me so that we get to know each other better. The smile on their faces let me know that they had favorably taken my act and conversation with professor Le Blanche.

There, Yasuhiro, I thought to myself, don't get mad at them. You are a stranger in this country. You had to pass some kind of test.

Yet, such situation could not make me content. Hypocrites and cowards are the last things I need for comfort in this world. I came to Paris to escape from them. But they exist in every corner of the world.

Although I knew her a little by sight (we did not even greet each other in passing by), I then looked more closely and more carefully at one rather short, supple girl, with a distinctly freckled face on which a turned-up nose stood prominently. Her hair was blond, slightly greasy and strewn in wisps all over her shoulders and down her back. She had a knitted ski cap on her head, and around her forehead she had tied a colorful band that held her hair. She wore a plaid windbreaker and tight, truly tight jeans, and she had suede ankle boots. An embroidered bag was hanging over her shoulder. There are thousands of girls like this in the streets at all times of day and night, but I have not kept my eyes on any of them for so long. As if my eyes were made of iron, and she was a magnet.

Without my own volition and intention, I had become a kind of hero since that day. My colleagues kept on patting me, saying some words which I interpreted as their support or delight with what I had done to the professor. It seemed that this must have made a very strong impression on them. Some would offer me to have a drink together at the nearest bistro, which I would skillfully and politely decline, justifying myself with the fact that I did not drink and that I had a scheduled telephone call with Tokyo at that time.

I remained alone. At least I thought so at first. The cadaver was prone on the table while professor Le Blanche was occupied with some books in front of an open glass cabinet in a smaller room.

I headed for the door, but a hunch told me that I was not alone in the room, and that there was someone else besides me nearby, upstairs, in the amphitheater seats, which were now in semi-darkness.

I turned around. Of course, in the middle of the third row was a girl with a ski cap on her head. She was leaning on the desk, her fists were supporting her chin, and she was looking straight at me.

I sensed a strange sign in that. I failed to interpret it to myself. But now it doesn't really matter, I thought to myself. There's a girl watching you and why do you need any explanation.

I had just recently noticed all the details on that girl. I dare to admit that I wanted to be around her. What I saw before me, I understood more as a gift from Buddha, and I felt uneasy and ashamed for having formed an opinion about it in advance. I was instantly overwhelmed by fear of how I would act in front of her.

But in that excitement and elation, it suddenly vanished. The enthusiasm did not let me be confused, something similar to the encouragement of a dear human being. A magic hand led me straight to her, towards the middle of the third row.

I went in between desks. I entered the fourth row, a step higher than hers, with the intention of being above her. I stopped right behind her. She turned and looked at me from below.

– I am Yasuhiro Tsuru-junior – I introduced myself. – Is that enough?

– That's too much – she replied. – I am Dominique Lemaire.

– Let's go somewhere for a panaché? – I suggested.

– Let's go somewhere for a panaché – she agreed.

As we were descending the staircase, she stopped. I turned around.

– Did you really lick your other finger? – she asked.

– I did not, really – I replied most frankly. – I lied to professor Le Blanche. I licked the same one I had stuck into that wretch. That's why we are going somewhere for a panaché to wash away the taste of the dead body. It's still in my mouth.

– I heard that you Japanese don't know how to laugh – she said. – You have no sense of humor, just like Germans, or like any hard-working and fanaticized nation.

– That's why we smile all the time – I replied to her.

I knew she did not understand me.

Paris, 27 February 1971

Possibly because of the long loneliness, I was already so poisoned with distrust in people that I could not even trust Dominique without thinking beforehand that her story was the most ordinary bluff. I know all too well that a bit of bluff and a bit of posing are enough for one solid theater. I have had enough of theater for quite some time; I had before my eyes my entire childhood and early youth, and I no longer needed it.

Since I have been with Dominique, some childhood images have started bothering me.

The stone rolls down the hill. I'm at the foot of it. I watch it. I watch it skip the smaller ones.

Suddenly, I find myself in a house. I am still in the same spot. Still at the foot of the hill. I notice that the house door is wide open. I would like to close it. I cannot even move it. I press the door handle and make a semicircle with the door. I feel the cold brass in my palm. I don't see the door now. I feel around. Everything is empty.

Then a sound roused me from my half-sleep.

Is it the ticking of the clock on the bedside table or the ringing of the phone in the apartment next door?

I am slowly coming back to reality. I'm upset. This is where fear begins to stir. I will not think about this dream. It's easier for me not seeing that horrible stone.

It would be so good if life were a dream.

The blink of an eye and everything, instantly, disappears.

I pulled my hands from under the covers. Neither was holding the handle, but my palms were still cold.

I looked toward the front door. It was there. Painted in brown varnish. The peephole in the middle. With a nickel-plated chain attached.

I am well-closed. Nobody can do anything to me.

I haven't had visions of my mother as often as I had in the first days upon my arrival in Paris. Our rare encounters in dreams had been leaving painful impressions on me, which, for a long time, kept me in a thrilling flicker so I physically felt my heart pounding and faltering.

The time spent with Dominique makes me pretty much stray away from it for now. I try to suppress those memories while I am around her, but at the same time, I want to avoid her suspicion and, consequently, a possible direct conversation on the subject. I would not give any significance to it if I thought of Dominique as a person who would be able to comprehend without affectation and bluffing with cheap and rapturous facial expressions and clichéd choice of words, which is likely to cause anger rather than comfort. Most often, listening to someone's confession means to listen while being silent. The hurt one needs no wise words, just silence.

I think the two of us cannot really talk about anything without manifestation of her parroty "blah-blah", superficial reaction, you Jassy imagine things, followed by a cascade of twenty or so trite phrases from Fromm, Marcuse, Cohn-Bendit and Sartre, but all so maladroitly garnished that I was bothered by these guys the moment she mentioned some of the names. I know that they were not to blame at all for the way their words affected my mind thanks to their advocate Dominique Lemaire.

From the very beginning of our acquaintance, I have been trying to look at myself from her perspective, looking at myself through her eyes. As for my relationship with her, there is nothing left for me but to admire her, starting to find her even beautiful, and for all she does, that she is *gentille et mignonne*[5].

I do not think I would be wrong to say that Dominique did indeed have something of a fragile plant in her. The strangest of all were her eyes, big and chestnut eyes, perhaps too big and heavy in relation to her tiny face.

One frosty, starry night, I woke up at two o'clock after midnight. I tried to remember if I was dreaming. I felt my throat was dry. I remembered there was a party inside me that night. And Dominique was there. I danced with her most often.

---

5 *Fr.* – Kind and cute.

I went to the bathroom. I poured water into a large glass. As I drank, my eyes accidentally stopped on the mirror.

Dominique + Jassy, it was written in red lipstick on its surface.

The handwriting could not have been hers. I know it well because I use her lecture notes. She must have been here and seen this. If she saw, why didn't she wipe it off. If she did not wipe it off, it means she did not mind it.

What a love syllogism!

For a while, I watched the letters on the mirror. The handwriting suggested that it was written by a female hand, probably with Dominique's blessing. If I don't mention anything to her tomorrow, she'll think I'm indifferent. I have to think carefully. Our first encounter will be at the lecture. It is not a good place for suavity.

Had I nothing to do with this, I would probably think it was the most outrageous outpour of pathos. Now I would not dare say it out loud, though it is not far from it. I repeat, I am so poisoned with distrust in people that it begins to fall on me as a considerable burden that I can hardly bear. I know that without it, people live more easily and comfortably. I cannot get rid of it completely, but it seems to me that I would feel some of the happiness, in an instant, if I would manage to free myself from it for at least a short while.

I have to try.

Paris, 5 April 1971

It's been fourteen days since I found myself before Dominique in a new role, clumsy and shy, which was normal for me anyway. It was constantly fluttering before my eyes while I was with her. Although I assured myself that in front of me was a mobile organic matter, such situation caused me considerable discomfort. Had I noticed that Dominique spotted it, I would have gotten rid of it fairly quickly.

And she either played dumb or it was her discreet gesture to have me relieved of it more easily.

I don't know, I don't know anything. All I know is that I felt nice and comfortable with her like I have never felt with anyone else. I wish she felt the same with me. For a long time, I was reluctant to ask her, but I did not muster up the courage to start a conversation on the subject.

Why think in the long run, especially about things like love. Is there anything more uncertain than that, as there is nothing more uncertain than hunger and death? And I'm a man who takes things dead seriously. I was sitting next to her, thinking: would it be better for us to live in Japan or here in France?

– Would you, Dodo, live in Japan? – I asked her, pretending to be joking.

– It's a pretty infantile question, whether you're kidding or talking seriously – she replied.

– I didn't mean it for my sake – I tried to lie to her. – I could have mentioned Chile or Kamchatka instead of Japan.

– You couldn't have – she replied quite offhandedly.

– Why not? – I wondered.

– Because you're neither from Chile nor from Kamchatka – she replied calmly. – What's bothering you? You don't have any plans with me, do you?

I am silent. She is silent too.

I understood from her silence that she caught me.

– Dodo, I guess we can talk about us?

The conversation, roughly, continued like this.

D: I CAN ONLY SPEAK OF LOVE IN FRONT OF A MAN
    CLOSE TO ME.

Y: DO YOU FEEL IT FOR ME?

D: I THINK NOT YET.

Y: IN THAT CASE, HOW COULD YOU GO TO BED WITH ME?

D: SOMETIMES I CAN LIE EVEN WITH THE ONE I DESPISE.

Y: I DON'T UNDERSTAND YOU, DODO.

D: LET'S NOT EVEN BOTHER TO UNDERSTAND MANY A THING. WHY DO WE NEED IT? ARE WE GOING TO BE HAPPIER IF WE DIAGNOSE THEM? YOU, FOR EXAMPLE, WOULD BE MUCH CLOSER TO ME IF YOU WOULD EXPERIENCE WHAT YOU'RE EXPERIENCING NOW WITH LESS SERIOUSNESS. I THINK LIFE IS FAR NICER AND EASIER IF ONE CUDGELS ONE'S BRAINS LESS ABOUT IT.

I was silent and listening to what she intended to say. I love her so much that her every word sounds convincing to me. She said all this with nonchalant hand gestures, obviously, without any need to think whether I would agree with that, or even whether I would be offended by that. However, at one point, it occurred to me that it would probably be more appropriate to crush that head that such words come from, which began to offend me so much that I accidentally, moving my hand across the coffee table, knocked the glass ashtray down. Luckily for me, it did not break on the floor.

– Well, you see, Jassy, an evil spirit could very easily conclude that you are unable to understand what one is telling you most candidly – Dominique said. – So, I'm asking you, to what purpose all this? We've been playing with adolescent questions for fifteen minutes now. Are we sitting here? Are we having a good time? I am, I don't know about you. Why bother with all these superfluous, boring and theatrical issues beforehand? We are starting to do math with ourselves, which is the last thing I would want to do. Relax, man, and enjoy, if you can enjoy next to me at all. You will have time to make your life shit. Merde!

Her every word awfully hurt me. Every single one of them jabbed like needles into my soul. I would have been happy had I been put in a situation to say these same words to her. If I continue like this, I believe that I will soon lose all of her respect.

She did not let me think in peace, for as soon as she had finished her coffee in one angry sip, she grabbed her bag from the chair and crossly threw it over her shoulder. At the door, she turned. She sized me up coldly and reprovingly: "I'm leaving. You screwed up royally for today."

– Where are you going? – I asked, surprised and ashamed.

– Is there anything more stupid coming from a man than choosing out of two billion women the freckled, ugly, blind as a bat, complex-ridden, loudmouth one for whom he will suffer. I'd be a hypocrite to let you sing such serenades.

– Wait Dodo – I tried to raise my voice – wait... As you see, I'm all confused. I'm afraid I might hurt you. Is there anything ugly in the fact that I love you?

– Love me, Jassy, as much as you want. Nobody can deny this right to you, but don't expect me to give you the same in return. Don't get any ideas. I've seen a lot of shit between my parents. First my father stabbed my mother to death with a knife, and seven years later, when they released him due to *illness*, in the same way he killed my older sister. If you mean to be serious with me, we can say: good night! to each other. Approach love the way we go to the cinema to watch a film – when the light turns on, you can feel the pleasure of having stolen two interesting hours from life. Capito, signor colonnello?[6]

– I don't get you at all – I replied.

– It is both good and terrible at the same time – she smiled. – In that case, look at things from this side. Is it that the Japanese see blurrily because of their slant eyes?

– So, what are my eyes like? – I was all wounded by her superiority, and on the right track to yield to her blows and mockeries.

– Your eyes are the most beautiful in the world – said unflappably the wide-opened door. – One is the color of beer in a green bottle, while the other is similar to a rolled-in-the-dust overripe sour cherry.

Then she furiously turned and walked down the hall. Instead of her, I looked at the bag swirling across her back, and then her back and bag and she got lost behind the exit door of the college.

Paris, 15 April 1971

I got up early this morning. I felt completely depressed. As I was lying in bed, I tried to remember my dream from the previous night. I have nearly forgotten it. What was left of it was a shattered and blurry image of my and Dominique's flight above the surface of a mountain lake, edged by dense antediluvian trees, the exotic thickness and height of which struck us with fear. She was under me, that is, I was riding on her. Only occasionally would she turn her head to the side because of the outburst of laughter that I couldn't even hear.

Peace reigned all over the place.

The color of the lake became brighter. Those huge trees suddenly vanished.

I couldn't remember anything else. A lump of pain lay in my chest.

---

6 *It.* – Do you understand, mister colonel?

I got up and went to the bathroom. I threw my pajamas off. Gymnastics was intended to chase away my somber and dogged mood. But already after the initial moves, this idea did not seem so amusing, that I, with bare limbs, would continue to flail my arms in the air. Hence, I turned on the strongest jet so that the cold water would bring me back to my senses.

After the first splashes, it seemed that I would succeed. The cold water was really refreshing and made me vigorous. I ardently tried to distract myself with objects around me so I wouldn't think about what was causing me an awful lot of pain.

So, I occupy myself with ordinary and almost imperceptible objects.

What the hell are these objects?

As much as I tried to make any kind of intimate contact with them, some devilish thread did neither leave me alone nor allow me to dismiss my thoughts about Dominique and her pressure to come to my place in the afternoon.

Why has she rejected my invitations for so long? She accepted this last one without my particular persuasion.

Is she tempting me or does she intend to satisfy her curiosity?

I do not believe I am right. In any case, she'll stop by for tea or sake, drink it and leave. Most often, things are far simpler than we imagine them to be. It would just be the best; I would put off all my doubts for another time. Perhaps it's best for a man to push all his questions aside? The hardest thing is to decide on an answer, especially for me, so confused and hesitant.

I just hope paranoia does not interfere with this whole dance.

Still, I have to be decisive. Just one moment. Then you see if your speculations are correct. Only then are we able to remove the veils from human faces and pull off their powdered masks. That's when you jump into the water and then say - hop! Indecisiveness creates uncertainty. With the decision, you shorten the path of dying, you avoid many anxieties in your soul. Man gets nothing if he takes refuge inside his skin like a sort of his own lair. From there, from that fortress of his, through those two glassy slits, he peeks, gawks and weighs with his precarious and mute experience. He undergoes all this fear and uncertainty in the illusion that he will eventually come out craftier and wiser. Life is short, usually boring, to have the patience to endure all of it without scream and anger within.

For a moment, I completely undressed. I went naked in front of the huge mirror in the hall. Did I truly need to spoil the already somber and dogged mood?

In the afternoon, I must buy high-heeled shoes, one suit with vertical stripes, and a few packs of cotton-wool pads for my shoulders to make them wider.

P.S. Whatever I wish for, what will happen to me is what is meant to happen to me.

Lundi, après le 15 avril 1971. ans.
Le minuit[7]

I: WHY DID YOU GO TO BED WITH ME?
D: TO MAKE MY HEART BEAT BETTER, MY BLOOD VESSELS EXPAND AND BLOOD FLOW FASTER, TO HAVE MY SKIN GET A NICE PINK COLOR, MY BRAIN FILL WITH BLOOD, TO HAVE SEX GET ME OUT OF MENTAL LETHARGY.

---

7 *Fr.* – Monday, after 15 April 1971, midnight

I: SO, YOU DIDN'T GO BECAUSE YOU FEEL SOMETHING FOR ME?

D: WHAT COULD I FEEL FOR YOU? I HAVE BEEN LIVING WITH A KIND OF SPIRITUAL AMNESIA FOR YEARS.

I: LOVE!

D: I FEEL FOR MY LOVERS THE SAME I FEEL FOR MY SHOES AS I TRY THEM ON IN THE SHOP; SOME ARE TIGHT, SOME ARE TOO BIG, AND SOME FIT ME PERFECTLY.

I: DO I FIT YOU?

D: JASSY, I THINK THAT YOU JUST INTEND TO ACT LIKE THE COMMONEST BRUTE, WHICH WILL NEVER WORK FOR YOU. YOU ARE JUST ONE STEP AWAY FROM RUNNING OUT INTO THE STREETS AND BRAGGING ABOUT ME AS A TROPHY.

(She took a cigarette from the pack. I did not even bother to light her cigarette. With a sad smile, she gave me a scornful look.)

D: LITERATURE AND FILMS HAVE TAUGHT YOU WRONG WHAT LOVE IS. AS THEY ARE WELL OVER HALF A CENTURY BEHIND THAT REAL, CONCRETE MAN, YOU HAVE MANAGED TO MIX UP THESE TWO THINGS WELL. FOR THE MOST PART, THE ONES WHO BULLSHITTED AND SCRIBBLED ABOUT THEM WERE THOSE WHO HAD BEEN DENIED THEM BECAUSE OF GOD KNOWS WHAT CIRCUMSTANCES. THEY ARE NO MORE. SOMETIMES I THINK THAT THEY NEVER EXISTED AT ALL, AND THE FACT THAT WE KEEP THINKING THEY STILL EXIST,

IS – I BELIEVE – AGAIN A MATTER OF THESE SAME MASTERS CALLED THE PENMEN. LES HOMMES DE LETTRES[8]. YOU DON'T KNOW WHAT'S BETTER - EITHER LIVING IN THAT KALEIDOSCOPE, BELIEVING THAT YOU WILL MANAGE TO DO THE SAME THING WITH YOUR LIFE OR LIVING THIS WAY WITHOUT MEANING AND PURPOSE. ANYWAY, I HAVE ALREADY BABBLED OUT A LOT TONIGHT. I DON'T LIKE BEING THE ONE WITH WHITE PIECES IN ANY KIND OF GABFEST LIKE THIS ONE ABOUT LOVE. MY FATHER ALSO PROBABLY HONESTLY THOUGHT THAT WHAT HE FELT FOR MY MOTHER WAS TRUE LOVE. HE WENT INTO MY GRANDDAD'S HOUSE AND POINTED HIS OFFICER'S GUN AT HIS DAUGHTER IN THEIR FAMILY PHOTO: EITHER YOU GIVE HER TO ME, OR YOU WILL NOT HAVE HER. THE MAN CONFUSED MATTERS OF THE HEART WITH PENIS AND VULVA, DIDN'T HE, JASSY?

I: DON'T CALL ME THAT. YOU EUROPEANS, YOU SUBJECT EVERYTHING TO YOUR OWN STANDARDS. YOU ARE UNABLE TO, AT LEAST FOR A MOMENT, LEAP OUT OF YOUR ARROGANT MENTAL CONFORMITY. HERE I AM, ALMOST CRAZY FROM MY FEELINGS FOR YOU AND YOU TRAMPLE ON IT ALL IN ORDER TO PERFORM THE SHODDIEST OPERETTA OUT OF IT.

D: JASSY, I REALLY HAVE NO INTENTION OF MOCKING THAT. I SPEAK ABOUT WHAT I FEEL. WHOSE FAULT IS IT THAT YOU GREW UP WITH PEOPLE WHO

---

8 *Fr.* – Men of letters

DISGUISED THEIR HATRED OR INDIFFERENCE WITH A PROFESSIONAL SMILE! HAVEN'T YOU ALREADY BECOME DISGUSTED WITH ME FOR MY EROTIC TREATISES AND DISCOURSES? IF YOU WERE TO SAY THE SAME TO ME, I WOULD HAVE PICKED UP A LONG TIME AGO AND LEFT YOU FOREVER. I, JASSY, AM NOT A CHICK FOR YOU. IF YOU WANT, I CAN GET READY AND LEAVE WITHOUT ANY ANGER RIGHT NOW. I'M HERE BECAUSE I WANT TO BE WITH YOU. DON'T EVER REACT TO SINCERITY, EVEN IF IT IS ABOUT PERVERSITY, NYMPHOMANIA... AS THE PURISTS DO WITH THEIR ORAL STORAGE OF LEARNED LABELING. SO, JASSY, FEEL FREE TO SAY THAT I'M A BITCH.

I: I HAVEN'T SAID THAT, NOR SHALL I EVER SAY IT.

D: YOU'RE A LIAR AND A COWARD, AND NOT SHY AND SCARED FOR ZEN AND SOME OTHER METAPHYSICAL REASONS, AS WE STUPID WESTERNERS TALK THROUGH OUR HAT ABOUT YOU. YOU DON'T EVEN HAVE THE GUTS TO TELL A BITCH THAT SHE'S A TRUE BITCH.

I: DODO!

D: I AM A BITCH DODO. I AM NOT MADEMOISELLE LEMAIRE[9]. I AM LA CHIENNE LEMAIRE[10].

I: I DO NOT INTEND TO DIRTY MY MOUTH WITH SUCH PROFANITIES.

D: IN THAT CASE, YOU'D BETTER MASTURBATE AND FEED YOUR MISERABLE IMAGINATION, AND LEAVE

---

9 *Fr.* – Miss Lemaire

10 *Fr.* – Bitch Lemaire (vulg.)

YOUR MORALS TO PAPER. PLEASE SET ME FREE FROM IT SO I WOULDN'T HAVE TO VOMIT. I HAVE MET MILLIONS OF MORALISTS OF ALL CALIBERS AND COLORS, WHO ARE VILER THAN JACK THE RIPPER HIMSELF.
AND NOW I'VE REALLY HAD ENOUGH OF YOU FOR TODAY!

She began to pick up the scattered things from the floor and chair. I intend to follow her, with a sense of powerlessness to tell her anything clever. I intend to tell her something, but it seems to me, and I'm afraid, that it will infuriate her even more, this time - forever. The only thing left to do is watch her in front of me half-enraged, ridiculously half-naked, and picking up an armful of her things. Hastily and carelessly, she got dressed along the way.

– Wait, Dodo, please – I tried to grab her by her biceps, but she roughly pushed my held-out hand.

– Don't you touch me! – she yelled.

– Well, we can't do that – I blurted just for the sake of saying something. – You still mean something to me.

– Listen, you midget, you can only lock the door behind me and we're done.

– Satan himself brought you to me to make fun of me. If only you knew how much I thought about it. Not a single night goes by that I do not dream of you in the most beautiful ways; do you know how much I talk with you in this same room and thus hurt myself so. When you happen to dream like this, you will have the right to make of me what you want.

– You already gave that right to yourself, didn't you? – she asked.

Some blind force moved me, and I headed straight for her.

– Yasuhiro! – she opened her eyes wide at the tiger that was now ominously approaching her. – Jassy!

– Yes, I am Jassy, crazy Jassy, craziest Jassy! Crazy Jassy...

She ran to me with her arms stretched, but as soon as I felt them around my neck, I saw her mouth curving, her eyes fading, and she soon slumped onto my chest. Her forefinger nail got stuck to one stitch of my sweater. I recalled from the books that the dying usually say something.

At that moment Dominique collapsed at my feet. It looked as if I were Christ and she was about to wash my feet as a sign of devotion and humility.

Her mouth could no longer babble and utter those horrible words.

I walked to the sofa to lie down for a bit. I felt my poisonous wrath going somewhere and spilling. Vanishing. Evaporating... I don't feel sorry for her at all. I even take pride in having done it at last.

– I killed Dominique! I killed Dominique! – I whisper in silence as if preparing for the theater play.

– I feverishly await a bite of conscience, but it just isn't coming.

– You, Jassy, have no conscience.

I don't know whether I'm saying it myself or Dodo is complaining about it.

Dominique is sitting like a discarded half-empty bag at the leg of the table.

– Man, you murdered Dominique Lemaire! – I said to myself.

– You killed, so what? – another voice replied. – They have committed thousands of murders of you as well so far.

I believe I am not insane. I look around. I am all alone in the room. I move my fingers and say to myself that I move my fingers. Professor Etiamble taught us in clinical neuropsychiatry that insanity is an *inadequate reception of the stimuli from the objective reality.*

Am I receiving the stimuli inadequately now?

I move my fingers and say to myself: "Yasuhiro, you're moving your fingers now!"

It will soon be two o'clock. I need to finish my diary entry for today. It is the sixteenth of April. I killed Dominique on the fifteenth. I must lie down and pull myself together. I will also think about what to do with the corpse. The most important thing is not to let them find me. The rest is less important.

Paris, 20 April 1971

I intentionally did not turn on the light. For a while, I stood in complete darkness, then reached the window, drew the curtain open and looked down the street. I feel how I begin to stiffen with fear. How much more courageous and peaceful I was yesterday with any consequences of what I had done to Dominique. At one point, I thought, even decided, to report to the police myself. I wouldn't be able to do that today. An immense fear crept over me. That's it, present in me, so I feel physical pain from it.

I am alone. Powerlessness and emptiness. I wish I could put my hand on something solid. I see that nothing comes my way as a mainstay. Everything escapes from me. Things are moving away as ghosts. As long as I can remember, it has always been like that. As if such cursed fate were intended for me.

I tried, near the window overlooking the street, to find answers to certain questions. I doubt that I can deceive myself with any of them.

What am I now? Neither man nor animal. I look like man but I am not him anymore.

How did all that happen with lightning speed?

I did not mean to kill Dominique. She made me do it. Doesn't she know that because of jealousy I used to wet my pants and take a lot of beatings for it?

Could it not be an extenuating circumstance for me?

I loved you most sincerely, Dodo, in you I saw not only a woman; you presented for me the possibilities to finally begin to correct things in myself that had taken an ominous course and that I had resisted for so long.

I found a candle in between the sheets. For a long time, I looked for the matches in the apartment. Finally, I found one on the fridge. I lit it against the glass.

The candle illuminated only one part of the room. Dominique is in the bathroom now. She is curled up like a fetus in the womb. I barely managed to pack her in my suitcase. Dominique weighs only forty-eight kilograms.

I remember that on one occasion the two of us weighed ourselves together in front of the Gare du Nord. She then said to me: "Jassy, I lost more weight", to which I added: "Now you're my true snowflake!"

The snowflake now lies in the suitcase and refuses to melt...

Paris, 20 April, around noon

Out of the corner of my eye, I watched two policemen. Neither paid attention to me and my suitcase. Around noon, I called a taxi. I ordered the driver to take me to Croissy-sur-Seine. When we got there, I paid for the ride, and then continued down the dirt road to the Seine. Out of excitement and fear, I could almost no longer carry the suitcase. It was not possible that my snowflake was inside. A real giant was certainly lying in it now.

I was darting glances around. In the immediate vicinity, on a downed tree, I noticed a couple of middle-aged lovers. She flirtatiously pushed him away with her hands, and he, blinded with lust, intended to take off her panties and, without taking their coats off, make love to her. The man was slightly younger than the woman. It was obvious he had a black wig on his head. I certainly wouldn't have noticed it, had it not moved aside and revealed a part of his bald head.

I smiled for the first time in the past four days.

It wouldn't truly be wise to leave her here. Someone could discover her at any moment. Then I felt my shirt sticking to my sweaty body.

I walked on. After about a hundred meters or so, I met a man with a huge blond beard covering his chest all the way to his belly. It seemed as if, before having a meal, he had tied a bib around his neck.

The man was sitting by the riverside. With pieces of bread he was taking pâté out of a can.

He looked at me. I instantly got confused. He smiled as if he wanted to encourage me.

I wonder what he thinks about me. Perhaps that I am a virtuous man?

These days, I get confused by an ordinary tree let alone by a living man, who, in addition, looks directly at me and my suitcase. It seems that my suitcase was not in the least suspicious to him as he did not see fit to give it a somewhat longer or closer look.

I almost nodded at him in greeting, but he had already turned.

Lucky man. Unlike Yasuhiro Tsuru-junior, he doesn't cudgel his brains into which bush to throw the suitcase with the corpse. Man often does not know that happiness is at his fingertips. Happiness is to have nothing to do with corpses.

I quickly dismissed the idea of renting a boat, paddling to the middle of the river and throwing my suitcase there as being rather naive, since at least a dozen witnesses saw me coming to this place. Even a blind man would be able to confirm that I was Japanese.

Our damn faces and our slant eyes. As if we had clothespins on our temples.

$$\frac{\sin x}{\cos x} = 1$$

I took the train back to Paris. As I traveled, I looked out the window at the Seine, the groves along its banks, and I had nothing else in my mind but hidden places where I could take Dominique.

I was roused from these daydreamings by the voice of the conductor, who asked to check the tickets. He then saw the luggage and asked me if it was my suitcase. I hesitated a little, then confirmed as casually as possible, nodding two or three times. He kindly requested that the suitcase be paid for as well: "Such is the regulation, sir!"

I quickly took the money out. Then a woman entered the compartment. She put her bag right next to my suitcase.

A gruesome thought popped into my mind. If I ate Dominique, no one would ever be able to find out what happened to her. No one would be able to prove that I killed her. I should not be queasy about it. I proved it in the pathology exercise.

After all, I think Dali has stated somewhere that cannibals devour the ones they love. So, he says, he could eat his Gala for love.

I looked around. I noticed with considerable discomfort that the woman was watching me with curiosity.

Watch me - I thought - as much as you want, as long as the stench does not spread from the suitcase.

I got off with the rest of the passengers at the Saint-Lazare. I looked at the clock, it was past four. I'll have to wait for midnight. Then I will probably be able to get rid of the suitcase.

It would be so good to put it in one of those huge hydraulic presses used to compress car wrecks into a small square mass. "Paris-Match" wrote that the Italian mafia encases its corpses in slush concrete.

God, I wish I could die! I'm such a coward that I even dare not kill myself.

It was pretty dark when I headed to Luxembourg park with my luggage. I went inside. I saw benches full of different guys. I sat on one. I was at the very end. I put the suitcase by my feet, to the left of the bench.

Only then did I feel how much fatigue had accumulated in my legs and arms.

I felt the newspaper in my inner pocket. I remembered picking up the *Asahi Shimbun* at one of the side newspapers shops at the Place de Clichy. I could kind of run my eyes over the letters under the light of a miserable lamp.

In every possible way I tried to concentrate on the headlines. They didn't bother me as much as that slew of smiling faces. They were all neatly combed, with their mouths wide open and a row of ultra-white teeth. Mostly false, of course.

I felt like tearing everything into tiny pieces.

I would certainly have done it, had the horoscope not caught my attention. I was interested in what the astrologist had to tell me for the week.

I found the Taurus. *You are certainly not wasting your time. Thoughtfulness is not your trait. But it is important to be understood.*

As I most earnestly tried to figure out the meaning of my horoscope in my unenviable situation, two men sat beside me on the bench at the same moment. One of them had a female wig on his head. That he was a man was obvious by the mighty biceps and triceps of his arms.

The two of them turned lustfully to each other, without looking back at me as if I were just an ordinary lath on the bench. I thought I heard: "Giapponese!"

If I heard right, then he must have been Italian. With the two of them embraced, it seemed to me that I could leave completely unnoticed. Thus, I intended to take advantage of such a lucky situation, if there even could be any luck at all about what was related to me. But just as I moved a few steps away, that transvestite with the female wig called me in a hermaphroditic voice: "Hey!"

I turned as if being pulled by ropes.

- Signor, é vostro questo bagaglio?[11]

Although I did not understand what he wanted to tell me, I mechanically remembered his question, assuming, based on my knowledge of French, that he intended to warn me about the forgotten suitcase.

Damn suitcase and Dominique in it. As if she were mocking me from inside?

I grinned at him and tapped my forehead as supposedly in 'where are my brains'. He grinned back at me, carefully looking all over my buttocks, but as if he didn't find anything interesting in my tiny body, he returned to his lover's embrace.

My throat was dry. I haven't eaten anything all day. I wasn't hungry, but I tell myself I completely got off track.

Is it accidental, or is it a subconscious desire to get so hungry so I can swallow Dominique more easily?

I'm in my little apartment again. I'm standing by the lit candle. I'm all sweaty. Soon the remaining part will melt in it.

I'm shivering. Thinking: here, you did something off-the-wall. You too finally became a murderer! And now what?

---

11 *It.* – Sir, is this your luggage?

I tried to inhale as much air as my lungs can receive, to fill all the bronchioles.

In vain. The weakness made me cling to the edge of the table.

I'm staring at some objects the contours of which I see in the semi-darkness. I startle. The distorted shadows frighten me. The semi-darkness frightens me. I want to transfer to another state. I don't want to be human anymore. It seems too disgraceful to me.

Am I thinking of death here?

I'm trying to think of something else. First, I recall professor Le Blanche. It's been a long time since I last saw him. I don't remember when the last time was I went to his lecture.

Clown Le Blanche. What happened with the corpse of that poor old man?

Nothing can distract my mind and thoughts from the suitcase still lying in the bathroom.

I am weak not so much from fear as from hunger and exhaustion for having not put anything in my mouth for two days. I'll make a pot of strong black coffee.

To wake me up... and then I will...

If I ate her by morning, would anyone be happier than me? The police are looking for you all over Paris, France. Interpol has been alarmed, and Dodo is flowing in my blood, I carry her in my bowels, and finally, in the simplest way, I expel her out of myself.

And I pull the toilet cistern cord.

I watched the dirty Seine yesterday. Who knows from what it is dirty. Who can prove that various Dominiques have not been dissolved there?

No one.

Dialectics. Panta rhei[12]. So, no one will be able to prove for me either.

Dialectics. The circulation of matter.

I poured water to the top of the pot. I'm sleepy. I can barely stand. Coffee will wake me up. I won't even add sugar, let it be as bitter as can be.

I couldn't find the matches for a long time. I felt my pockets. I did not dare to press the electrical switch. If any bulb on the pendant came on, I think I would go crazy that very instant. I don't like the light. Darkness is more pleasant for me.

I couldn't find any matches at all. I looked for them around the candle. They were not there either. I feel like I have to drag my feet. I haven't slept in two nights. If I could doze off just a bit, I think I would feel like a new man. I'll set the alarm clock. Perhaps it would be better to bestir myself a little?

I remembered leaving the matches this morning on the inside windowsill.

I felt them in the dark. The box slipped and dropped onto the floor. I bent down to retrieve it. It made my head swim. However, I remained conscious, only to realize that I had banged my head hard against the edge of the table.

When my head cleared, I went to the stove to turn on the gas. Then I put the pot on the pan support.

I have neither strength nor will to wave my hand to wake myself up.

I look at the clock. It's almost half past two. In two to three hours it will be morning. This is the day I will finally get rid of the suitcase. I must. I absolutely must. There is no doubt about that I lie down. I'm waiting for the water to boil. I feel a terrifying force pulling me to the

12 *Gr.* – Everything flows, nothing stands still (the saying of the ancient Greek sage Heraclitus).

bottom, to the promised paradise spaces. It pulls me for a while, then stops, then lulls me on the spot, cools my boiling-hot cheeks, closes me in, and then breezes over my eyelids. From afar I can see it putting its finger vertically in front of its mouth and letting me know to keep quiet and not say anything.

– Shhh!

3.

On that day, the twenty-first of April, police investigator Jean Moulin will have interrogated Japanese national and medical student Yasuhiro Tsuru at the Quai d'Orsay on suspicion that he may have been the killer of French national and medical student Dominique Lemaire. Any questioning about the suspect's mental state inevitably raises certain side issues: are events in the life of man the result of his planning or do they take place independently of his volition and control.

Yasuhiro Tsuru showed certain signs of derangement before the investigator, which he naturally sought to justify – adroitly or maladroitly – by the signs of illness that chronically sets in during spring. It seems that criminals and police require a setting for their pieces. Faced even more with Dominique within himself, he suddenly felt tiny. After all, the killer too may very well have performed his play simultaneously with them, and realized his nerves began to fray. Yet perhaps even Dominique also unwittingly wanted such ultimate synthesis?

Upon arrest, Tsuru Yasuhiro was subjected to probably the most thorough hearing that was most eagerly conducted by the entire expert teams of police officers, lawyers, sociologists, criminologists, graphologists, and psychiatrists.

In the first six months of his confinement, he spent around nine hundred hours with psychiatrists alone; – six hours a day, six hours a week. Since no question of his guilt was raised – as Yasuhiro was arrested with his *evidence*, and later, in his apartment, police investigators found his diary describing the crime and what preceded the crime in detail – the investigation could focus on his mental identity and motives. The psychiatrists collected a wealth of information on what they thought was important to him and what he had stated before them that he thought about himself.

They knew almost nothing about his motives. About who he was and what he was, Yasuhiro spun a different story each day for months, which stories had not much to do with reality, in fact, had not too much to do with psychiatric and police records. They were waiting for him with them, as with a net into which he had to be lured and caught. The purpose of all his stories, it seems, was an attempt to obscure his personality as much as possible.

For example, when asked if he could describe his mother, then he seemed to describe himself. She was – he says – short, lean, dark-eyed, muscular, highly imaginative, of light brown complexion, agile, interested in skiing, she read only mystical and spiritualistic literature, had a rather complex attitude towards her husband, suffered from arteriosclerosis, asocial behavior, caring towards servants and intolerant of aristocrats.

Her son, the doctors also noted, on top of that, was "shortsighted" and astigmatic. He used both his right and left hand equally well. He had abnormally scanty hair on his body and his skin was unusually sensitive. For no apparent reason, he would suddenly get goosebumps. Still, he was always willing to undergo the pain-inducing tests. He had an eidetic memory: "he was given a puzzle of 412 elements, which he studied for three days, and then, blindfolded, he solved it in eleven minutes and twenty seconds".

The only test of the kind he could not solve was a puzzle in the shape of a human head.

In the first month of his sentence, Yasuhiro spent most of his time in bed. He would pull a blanket over his head and turn, facing the wall. Those interested, who observed him through a special peep hole, were not quite sure whether – he – did not, or did, pretend.

Epilogue

Ten years after that infamous event, the name of Yasuhiro Tsuru was once again dragged all over the front pages of the tabloids. Their older readers had the opportunity to ferret out of their memory the image of the *Ripper from Tokyo*, which in those days warned about him from the shop windows of all newspaper shops throughout France, and not just France. Police gave the newspapers news of his spectacular escape from La Santé Prison. After a few days of unsuccessful manhunt, using all available means, they reappeared, this time in France-Soir with an advertisement through which they offered a fantastic reward of FF 100.000 to anyone with information on any solid lead.

Theoretically and practically, in those days anyone could play with Yasuhiro's life, on the one hand, or with the zeal of the police, on the other.

During this time, he lived in the steep La Fontaine street, at number 12, just down from the Moulin Rouge. He languished away like a bat in the attic of an unsightly four-story building, provided by some guy who discreetly intercepted him on the metro, and whispered to him that he had received a secret order from his boss in La Santé to take him to a safe place until the "flics and scribes are over".

There is nothing left for Yasuhiro but to surrender himself to his angels, or to run straight into the hands of police just here in a public place like a Christmas tree for Christmas holidays. Many years of imprisonment with a wide variety of demimonde rogues taught him well that curiosity was not very desirable in such situations, even if his own skin was at stake, and he could not milk anyone for any information, because he did not have even a sou to his name. He was constantly troubled by the question of why they had chosen to help him of all people in Paris. So far, no one was indebted to him, nor had he fallen afoul of anyone.

Mulling over doubts about the venerable intentions of his saviors and current guardians, and finally, reproaching himself for his paranoia, he came up several times with the bold idea of escaping from his secret hiding place. However, in the end, he pulled himself together and immediately dismissed this idea as crazy and suicidal, seeing that he would get himself into even more trouble, if not in the open arms of the police themselves.

This way, he was at least hidden from their eyes.

After some time, the captions from the front pages of the yellow press moved to the crime sections, to a more inconspicuous place. The last piece of news said that the investigation was still ongoing.

In the meantime, Marc Chioffi, one of Yasuhiro's guardians, will have gone back on his promise of silence. Over the public pay telephone, anonymously and with a handkerchief over his mouth so that no one would recognize his voice, he left a message for a man from the police that a piece of paper with the current address of fugitive inmate Yasuhiro Tsuru could be found in a garbage bin about ten meters away of the place he was calling from.

Thanks to their experts in deciphering telephone numbers and lines, the police were notified that a message containing such content had been sent from Croissy. There was one telephone booth placed at the very end of the Gounod Avenue. A radio call was promptly made ordering the local commissariat to find the paper with the address in a garbage bin just about ten meters away from the telephone booth. They were soon notified in the same way that the call was not a prank and that everything was in its place.

La Fontaine 12, the fourth floor, attic.

Only half an hour later, the specified four-story building was surrounded by police. Over the loudhailer, they urged Yasuhiro to surrender peacefully. Everything was surrounded and not even a fly could escape unnoticed.

In view of this...

To this day no one knows for sure what saved Yasuhiro Tsuru. Was it the sloppiness or insufficient watchfulness of the police? The night? Or the rain that was bucketing down? His crazy courage that made his whole being consumed with swiftness as, like a dormouse, he fled across the rooftops of neighboring buildings?

And when he finally crashed from a low wall into one narrow street, he first stood there transfixed not knowing which side to turn to, and then with a smile he turned to the sky, pointing his forefinger upwards: "Old man, I'm forever in your debt!"

For the next three days, he was hiding in the Léningrad Street, in the studio of his medical colleague. The colleague warned Yasuhiro that he could stay there one week at the longest, mostly thanks to the fact that he had so "ingeniously thrust his finger into the asshole of that corpse and then licked it".

Yasuhiro listened to his babbling between the forty-fifth and the fiftieth cigarette. He asked Bernard to put one letter in the mailbox. It was addressed to the four-story building on La Fontaine street. He briefly and clearly told them that someday he would take his revenge on Marc Chioffi by personally ripping his parroty tongue out. He knew full well that Marc did it without anyone's knowledge and permission, because that was what kept all those unknown saviors from handing him over to the cops, like a bird in the cage, on the very first day. He could no longer remain in Paris; he thought that he needed to flee it as soon as possible. How and where to? – that was his problem. And he had one more problem: to rip his tongue out! Just that much.

The next day, at the crack of dawn, three men entered the studio and remained talking with him until noon. Yasuhiro was left to ponder their proposal. In the late evening, he looked for a soap and razor, and then carefully shaved his scruffy beard and moustache. He put on a new suit and walked out. As if no one was looking for him, he walked the city at a calm and steady pace, of course, watching carefully every suspicious movement around himself. He would only stop in front of the Pont Neuf where he used to pass by with Dominique a long time ago, holding her tiny, bony and always cool hand in his pocket. He had never been happier in his life than at that moment.

Though almost trapped by treason, he was not so blinded by hatred so as to put himself in danger by staying longer in Paris to settle some of his private accounts. He watched the Seine shimmering in places the light of the street lamps reached. He grinned and muttered to himself that he would leave such impressions for some better times when he will have returned to France as her hero and having his chest adorned with the Legion of Honor.

All trace of him was lost for a while. Those who thought they knew him were sure that, out of a sense of aristocratic honor towards himself, he most likely had performed seppuku.

While they speculated and bet on such possibilities, it had been a while since a note had been recorded in his file that he was in the Foreign Legion.

A year later, a photo of French legionnaires in Chad appeared in the midsection of one issue of the *Paris-Match*. The photo was taken with a secret telescopic lens. Due to the lack of reliable information or to the censor's concern for national pride, the reportage was published with scant and general information, with the photos enlarged to take up as much space as possible, leaving nothing but modest space and extreme skimpiness to the text itself. But even that was enough for some to have their subconscious doubts pushed forward.

The photo depicted a group of legionnaires at rest. On the left side, those who knew him could nicely recognize Yasuhiro doing pushups on the barrel of a cannon. It was a color photograph, and the presence of all races was readily observable. The only ones missing were Indians and Eskimos.

In the text, one sentence stood outside the general context of that whole short caption. It stated that the legionnaires, for becoming accustomed to the iron military discipline, slept for months in wooden huts on the hard-packed soil and in full battle gear.

The photographs, which were subsequently periodically published on the pages of the same magazine, later proved not to be credible. The reason for this may be the fact that most legionnaires categorically refuse to be photographed by anyone in an effort to preserve their secretiveness by such gesture.

In the second half of 1983, rumors spread among the legionnaires that they would soon be transferred to a battlefield outside Europe. They concluded this on the basis of the officers' kindness towards them, and that was the best sign that nothing good was coming their way soon.

– We'll be going with daddies to the carousel soon!

– To the *Napoleon* I want to go, to Caledonia or Beirut!

– Beirut has pussies and gold up to the knees!

– And blood and shit up to the throat!

– Whatever crap you do, with your shitty name you'll never be able to fill the five columns on the front page.

– We all came from the front pages straight to this legion.

– You can only get there now if you kill Mitterrand.

– They will write more about him than about me.

– You'll be a tiny footnote in his biography.

At the end of September, on the very border of Chad and Libya, on one Saharan dune, with a warm khamsin blowing over it, before the line of officers, the legionnaires shouted as one the solemn oath that they would "with arms, heart and mind protect France where needed".

Forty-eight hours after that, in the middle of the night, came the mobilization order. The legionnaires already knew to which "carousel daddies were taking them".

On the third day of the month of October, a battleship with legionnaires docked at the southern pier of the Beirut Port. In the distance, one could hear the sporadic dim volleys or rare isolated machine gun bursts. Light from the firing would for a moment illuminate the sky over Beirut, which was similar to the illustrations of heaven in biblical images. A few casual passers-by, looking askance, hastily counted those who, at that moment, were crossing the gangway to the stone pier. Those who closely watched them could count seventy-four legionnaires, five officers and one military adviser.

At the end of that strange column of eighty people, paired with one big black guy, walked Yasuhiro, the way that Ole and Axel strode side by side in the comedy films. The same smile, only this time somewhat glassy and snakelike. It would only then have been possible to conclude that it had never been there for the sake of cheerfulness of spirit, but simply assumed, kind and learned.

The Japanese smile.

In this somewhat quieter part of the city, the advertisements of numerous companies and shops were shining everywhere. The colors glittered and enticed the idle and the rich.

– Pussies and gold up to the knees, and blood and shit up to the throat – the black guy laughed hoarsely at Yasuhiro. "As a kid did you watch the movie – *The Beirut Nights?*"

Yasuhiro didn't even bother to understand what his buddy wanted to tell him. He had never mastered the finesse of French so that he could understand it even when disconnected from reality so as to listen with half an ear those who spoke that language. He could only do it with Japanese.

He indeed heard that the black guy babbled something with his saxophone voice, and he laughed at that, but couldn't detach himself from his momentary sweetness, to pain, to tears, to sadness, as through memories and foggy veil he put all his efforts to revive that bench on the bank of the Seine, he felt her little bony hand in his, in his pocket, their fingers intertwined and they squeezed them to be closer to one another.

And just as he was trying to revive that longing smile on Dominique's freckled face, a strange rumble, someone's mixed shouts, crying, and the black guy's saxophone roused him from his half-sleep. Only then did he snap awake and return to reality.

Israeli tanks were coming their way, and their planes began tearing the sky.

One morning, Yasuhiro got up early. Although he had shaved the previous night, he planned to go with the *Remington* over his chin once more to have it thoroughly shaved and totally smooth. Hence, he headed for the bathroom. As he was walking down the middle of the hall, he heard some rumbling similar to a quake. He felt the ground tremble from it. The light bulb was swinging on the ceiling, and before he could do anything, he saw with his own eyes a crack in the wall widening like cheese being broken off. The crack was getting so wide that the walls around him began to collapse. Yasuhiro thought of that detail as someone's joke or his nightmare, so he smiled to dispel that nightmare.

All over, the walls were crumbling, the plaster falling off them and the dust rising so he could not even see his own finger in front of him.

– What is this now?... – he thought. – An earthquake?

That same day, the world agencies released to the world the news of the dreadful explosion in Beirut.

A TRUCK FULL OF EXPLOSIVES CRASHED AT FULL SPEED INTO THE BUILDING HOUSING AMERICAN AND FRENCH SOLDIERS

First assumptions say that 200 Americans and 50 Frenchmen found their death under the rubble. The number of victims is feared to be higher.

The front pages of the first afternoon newspapers featured a report on the terrorist act of an organization called *Hezbollah*, which was of the pro-Iranian orientation. So far, no one had officially claimed responsibility for having organized that senseless act. The reportage on this was published in full five columns, along with a photograph showing a pile of stones and razed blocks.

The following day, at about eleven o'clock local time, rescue crews pulled from the rubble the upper half of the body of a thirty-year-old, youthful-looking man, whose identity could not immediately be determined. His other, lower part of his body lay crushed under a stone block. Nothing could be said about the young man at that moment. The only assumption, made on the basis of his characteristic physiognomy, was that he was a Japanese. Which citizenship he had, which army he had served, will have subsequently been identified by the lists, which were still to be received from the American and French military commands, since the Japanese government had not sent its military contingent at all.

About The Author:

Sead Mahmutefendić was born in Sarajevo in 1949. He attended primary and high school in Konjic, and the Faculty of Philology in Belgrade.

He worked as a high school professor and librarian in Sokolac, Rijeka and Sarajevo.

Member of the Croatian Writers' Association and the Association of Writers of Bosnia and Herzegovina.

Writer, novelist, short story writer, essayist, poet.

His works have been published in the panoramas and collections of Eastern European and South Slavic literatures, the anthologies and chrestomathies of contemporary Croatian prose, and Bosnian-Herzegovinian and Bosniak prose and poetry.

He is the author of more than thirty books. Among them stand out the novels *Kelvin's Zero, Placebo: The Beauty and Horror of Lies, The Man Who Spits on His Own Grave, Teasing (of) Salko Pirija, Fish and One-Eyed Jack, The Centrifugal Citizens, Demons, How Japanese is That, Like in a Movie, The Place Where Someone Ate a Flower*, and the books of columns *A Memorandum for the Reconquista, The Big and Small Cannibals, Onanism of Death of Life, A Framework for Some Other Reality*, as well as dozens of short stories, essays, columns, poems and book reviews. So far, his literary work comprises over eighty volumes. His selected novels were published twice, in 2 volumes in 2005, and Collected novels in 15 volumes in 2020.

He has won multiple awards. He was nominated twice for one of the most prestigious literary awards in the world, the IMPAC Dublin Award (2016 and 2020). He also won the Skender Kulenović Award.

Some of his novels, poems and poem cycles as well as short stories have been translated into a dozen languages.

He is the author of a series of psychological novels, stories and essays, characterized by unbridled and hyperdynamic style, tones of black humor, and a growing atmosphere of threat. Through variation of lyrical and naturalistic elements and depiction of marginal characters, he continues with his fantastic naturalism by counterpointing the poetics of absurdity and documentary verism. He has written works in which he did not deviate from his beliefs as much as was possible, and he circumvented censorship with the help of metaphor. Due to his prolific literary production of publishing at least one and sometimes two titles in a year (since 1991), and even three titles in 2000, critics describe this unusual phenomenon as the endurance of a Late-Victorian writer along with a linguistic life fervor. The results of his literary strategy have been a behind-the-scenes look, which often has a bitter taste of shock and horror over the fragility and impermanence of man's ethical values.

Lightning Source UK Ltd.
Milton Keynes UK
UKHW010706240520
363742UK00004B/119/J